# Bounced: A Blue Collar Bad Boys Book

**Blue Collar Bad Boys, Volume 1**

Brill Harper

Published by Brill Harper, 2017.

This is a work of fiction. Similarities to real people, places, or events are entirely coincidental.

BOUNCED: A BLUE COLLAR BAD BOYS BOOK

**First edition. September 4, 2017.**

Copyright © 2017 Brill Harper.

ISBN: 978-1729379295

Written by Brill Harper.

Sexy bad boys who do sexy bad things with their rough hands and the innocent virgins who love them. What's not to like? Sign up for Brill's Bites[1] so you never miss a new release. I won't spam you—I don't have time! You'll only get emails from me when there is a new release or a really great sale.

---

1. http://eepurl.com/cP0AZr

# About this Book

### Anvil

They call me Anvil.

It's not my real name, but that's what it feels like when my meaty fist comes down on you if you misbehave in the road house where I work.

I've seen some crazy stuff as a bouncer. I thought I'd seen it all.

But I've never seen anything like her. Just one look and I knew my life was never going to be the same.

She's sweet, innocent, and looking for trouble.

She found it.

I'm big and mean and more trouble than she ever imagined. I'm going to mess up all her carefully laid plans. And I'm going to make her mine.

### Sarah

I'm a careful girl. Life is too dangerous not to be. I have a plan. Goals. And none of them include an overly-muscled, tattooed, possessive bouncer with an eye patch from the road house just outside of city limits.

I just wanted one night off from being perfect, boring, and careful.

He's too much man for a girl like me. Too intense. Too visceral.

But I don't think he's going to let me go.

Author's Confession: I don't even know if this could happen in real life. Luckily, it's a book. That means the hot, tatted, beardy bouncer can totally take one look at the virgin college student studying actuarial science and know he's going to marry the sh!t out of her. Right? Anyway—totally safe romance-HEA, no cheating, hero wouldn't dream of looking at another woman after he sees Sarah. Trust Auntie Brill. It's a crazy story, but it's so much fun.

# Chapter One

## Sarah

This is the worst idea I've ever had. Times one million. Maybe times a million more than that.

Christa and I are following a completely bald three-hundred-pound bouncer named Jim through the back door of Billy's Suds. It's a service entrance, and from what I've gathered, Christa has offered a service in exchange for letting us drink as if we were twenty-one.

When she told me she could get us in, she didn't mention anything about this part of it. She comes here all the time, she said. She always gets in, she said. Never a problem...well, you get the idea. I didn't ask how or why they always let her in. It seems to me, if there were this kind of exchange, it ought to have been worth mentioning. Like, "I can get us in because I give the bald guy named Jim a beej every Tuesday night."

Billy's Suds is a road house just outside of city limits. It smells like smoke and urine, to be honest. And the floor is sticky as we walk down the dark paneled hallway into a room marked *Office*. I don't want to know what the sticky substance is. Billy's Suds is the kind of place where it's better not to ask. I will probably throw my shoes away when I get home.

My stomach acid is rolling to a boil, and I'm trying to act cool but doubt that it's working. I mean, come on. This is not me. Not my life. Not even what I'd willingly watch on TV. I go to bed at ten and get up at six. I eat five servings of fruits and vegetables every day. I don't smoke. I don't drink. I turn my college assignments in early.

I do not follow strange men through back doors of illicit bars. I have never given a beej before, and I'm hoping to keep that record going at least this one more night.

Jim opens the door and ladies-firsts-us into the room, closing the door behind him. It smells like more smoke, but less urine in here. That's all I can say for it. I hadn't expected a backstage tour of the road house, and under other circumstances, I might have been more intrigued since the reason I was here tonight was curiosity.

Normally, I'm a good girl. I follow the rules. Rules made by other people and rules I make for myself. Like, I might even say rule-following is my super power. I'm studying actuarial science because I think it's fun. That's how risk averse I am.

But I've been feeling sort of...restless...lately. I thought maybe if I did something just a little crazy, a little less me, I could shake it off. Feel normal again.

I wanted to go to a bar. See it. Order a beer. Maybe even drink it. I didn't plan anything too illicit. This is way off my radar of acceptable. But Christa is smiling like she just got asked to prom, and Jim looks oddly goofy about it, too.

As if I'm not in the room, he asks Christa, "Is this a twofer, or is she just a watcher?"

My breath freezes. I'm not wild about either opportunity. But for the love of God, *watcher, please say watcher*.

Christa flips her long, blonde hair over her shoulder and reaches for his zipper. "I'm all the woman you need tonight, Jim."

"You sure, baby?" He's looking at me, so I think he's asking me. But Christa is sliding to her knees, and I don't know where else to look so I nod quickly and move to a wall that holds some pictures and framed news stories about tournaments and things. I pretend they are supremely interesting and try to block out the sound of slurping and a long, happy groan from Jim.

I have never felt so awkward in my life. I'm hugging myself and repeating a litany in my head about how this will all be over soon. *All be over soon. All be over soon.*

"Thought you said she wanted to watch?" he asks Christa. "She get off on that? She's not even looking."

Every square inch of my skin is red hot and blazing. There's a window, and I'm contemplating throwing myself out of it.

"Leave her alone, Jim. She's sweet," answers Christa. "I just wanted to get her out for a bit. She's my tutor."

"Ah, baby. You could tutor her. Nobody slobs a knob like you do, princess."

I wince. Shakespeare Jim is not. But at least he's appreciative.

I wonder if it would be too obvious if I plug my ears and start humming "Mary had a Little Lamb" because, while I'd seen some pretty epic blow jobs on my Tumblr page, this voyeurism thing isn't working out for me. All I feel is a supreme case of embarrassment.

This is real life. This is totally happening. I should be home with Netflix and takeout. I was not made for road house sex listening.

The door opens, and I hear it slam as it bounces off the wall behind it.

Jim yells, "Occupied!" as I turn to face the commotion.

Commotion indeed.

You would think, in a normal situation, the eyes would be drawn to the blonde on her knees with a cock in her mouth. But no. People having sex is not the biggest thing happening in the room. Sorry, Jim. No offense.

What's riveting is the giant standing in the doorway with hellfire in one eye and a patch over the second with a long angry scar slashing his left cheek. His hands are pulled into fists. Really big, meaty fists. He spares a glance at Romeo and Juliet and then focuses his dark gaze on me.

I feel like I'm on a stage under a hot spotlight. It's maybe just a moment, but I swear the only thing I can here is his breathing. Like time is standing still except for the two of us.

"Oh my God," Christa squeals and breaks the stillness. She crabwalks away from Jim as he tries to stuff himself back into his pants. I help her up while the big guy in the doorway moves in to the room.

I'm sure I've never been in the presence of so much testosterone. The two men in this small office with us are huge. Jim outweighs Patch Guy, but only because Patch Guy is all muscle while Jim is...well, Jim is not in as good of shape.

The differences don't end there. Jim is bald; Patch Guy has a full head of hair. They are both covered in tattoos. Patch Guy has sleeves made of them. They are both men I wouldn't want to run into in an alley or be trapped in a tiny office with. There's this crazy energy in the room. The kind of tension that comes right before a lightning strike. The hairs on my arms and back of my neck are quilled up like a porcupine.

"What are you doing here tonight?" Jim asks the tree trunk who looks like he's about to beat the shit out of him. "You're off."

"I told you enough with the minors, man," Patch Guy replies. "You're going to get fired. You want a blow job, ask her out on a date someplace you don't work. Now she's bringing friends?" He stalks over to me and yanks my purse out of my hands, ignoring my indignant utterings. He pulls my wallet out, finds my I.D. and throws the rest onto the floor. He looks at it, looks at me, looks at it again. "You've got to be fucking kidding me."

He spins back to Jim. "This is the last time I cover for you. Get back on the door and do your job." To Christa, "I don't see you here again until your birthday or I call the cops myself. We clear?"

She nods. She's unusually pale, so her overdone eye makeup makes her eyes look like she's some kind of blonde anime character.

"Go the fuck home," he tells her.

Christa puts her head down and scurries with purpose to the door. Jim is already out of the room, presumably back to work. I need to go with Christa; she's my ride. But my stuff is on the floor and if I go down there and get it, I'll be...well, down there with the Patch Guy's junk. He seems to figure out my hold-up and takes two steps back. I gather my wallet and stuff it back in my purse, then get up and hold out my hand for my license.

He shakes his head.

Really? He's keeping it? Can he do that?

I swallow. "Please." My eyes go to the door. Christa is in the hall waiting. Thank goodness. "I need to go with her. She's my ride."

He's staring at me like we're in some kind of interrogation battle that I would so lose. If I had secrets, I'd be spilling them right now. Luckily for me, I don't ever do anything worth hiding. He can save that fierce glare for someone else.

Without looking over his shoulder at her, he says, "I said go the fuck home, Christa. Don't make me say it again."

I plead to her with my eyes not to leave me, but she looks real sorry before she shrugs and darts out of my line of sight.

Fine, he can keep my license. I'm so outta here. I take two steps, but he blocks my exit. "Don't think so."

"Look, I haven't done anything wrong." He snorts. "Yet," I add. "The office is not off-limits to minors, and I haven't set foot in the bar or had a drop of alcohol."

"That's some fine argument for the court. You going to law school?"

I shake my head. "I'm a finance major. But I know my rights. You can't keep me here."

"Not legally, no."

I exhale deeply. Good. That's settled. I try another step, but this time, instead of just blocking me, he steps *into* me and puts the distance between our bodies at zero inches. His hands rest heavily on my shoulders. I don't think he's pushing them down, they are just heavy because they are so big.

I tilt my head up. Way up. His expression hasn't softened at all. He's looking at me with some seriously fierce intensity. The scar, the tattoos, the eye patch, the strength all combine into this man who seems more primordial than not.

I concentrate on keeping my voice even. "I thought we just agreed you have no legal reason to keep me here." *Don't panic.*

"Yep."

"Then please let me pass."

"Baby, you're not going anywhere."

# Chapter Two

## Anvil

I am not a good man. But I am an excellent cooler—bar bouncer. A place like Billy's needs strong leadership for its security staff.

We don't have it.

So I do the best I can. The management might not be great, but it's not the worst place I ever worked.

I try to keep the problems on ice, but Jim is crazy about that damn chick. He's a good bouncer otherwise. He just can't keep his dick in his pants when it comes to Christa. She could cause us all kinds of problems, but he has a real weakness for her mouth.

And because of that, now I have a new problem. One that is testing my stone-cold self.

"Baby, you're not going anywhere," I tell the sweet thing watching the exit.

She's looking up at me with those eyes all wide and a little scared, and I am getting off on it. She is trembling, and she should be. She walked into the wrong bar tonight. I want to terrify her. I *want* her to be nervous and anxious and scared as fuck.

Because she has scared the fuck out of me.

"Explain this shit," I say, finally handing her back her driver's license.

She squirrels it into her purse like I might try to take it back. "I'm not sure what you're asking, but I need to go. Really."

I don't think so.

"Why won't you let me go?"

That's a good question. But not the first one I want answered. "Why did you sneak into Billy's tonight?"

"Why does anyone sneak into a bar?" She gives up watching the door, knowing Christa is long gone by now, and slumps against the desk. "Were you never underage? Was this not something your generation did, too?"

She startles a chuckle out of me, and I don't startle or chuckle easily.

I'm only ten years older, but maybe I've packed a lot of hard living into those years.

She's a cheeky little thing. Not sure when she decided she wasn't afraid to be alone in the room with me, though. "Baby, you couldn't wait for twenty-seven hours? Your birthday is the day after tomorrow."

She shrugs.

Not good enough. "What kind of girl waits to sneak into a bar until she's *almost* old enough? You could have come tomorrow at midnight."

"What makes you think this is my first time?"

"You've got cherry written all over you." When she blushes an angry shade of pink, I realize I hit my mark times two. A virgin. No fucking way.

Now I really am scared of her.

This girl is a baited trap.

I'm not a guy who believes in love, so I sure as hell don't believe in love at first sight. But something happened. Something changed. I don't know what to call it, how I feel. How I felt when I first laid eyes on her. It was primal. Like I zeroed in on her scent. I may not believe in love, but I do believe we are all just animals. And this beast just discovered his mate.

Knowing I'll be first makes it all the better.

Fuck me, but I think I'm going to be her last, too.

"My name is Anvil," I tell her.

She tilts her head at me. Narrows her eyes a bit. "No, it's really not."

My God, this little slip of a thing is going to be my downfall. "That's what they call me." I make a fist. "That's what these feel like."

She does this twisty thing with her lips. Like re-runs of The Church Lady on *SNL*. Only, damn if I don't think it's sexy, her little judgement of me. She likes clutching pearls so much, I'd be happy to give her a pearl necklace.

"What's your real name, Anvil?"

The air gets thick between us. I'm feeling like we're about to do a super slow motion fight scene from *The Matrix*. Only I don't want to fight this girl. I think I want to marry her.

This is the most fucked up day.

"Nobody knows my real name," I say, putting off the inevitable. I'm going to tell her my real name. I'm going to *give* her my last name. I'm going to give her babies and any damn thing she ever wanted. Who is this woman that could bring me down so hard and so fast?

"I want to know it," she says simply.

"Melvin," I reply.

She quirks those lips into another wry smile. "That's...well this has been a really strange night, hasn't it? I need to go now, *Melvin.*"

"I hope you're still laughing when I make you Mrs. Melvin Cartwright."

She inhales sharply, and I feel some relief at not being the only one tits up in this conversation again.

"I'm getting ahead of myself. I told you my first name, now you tell me the real reason you are out two days before you turn twenty-one sneaking into bars."

"Well, Melvin..."

"Careful, baby girl." My voice sounds a little deeper, a little more gravel in it than usual. I think it grated across her little raw nerves a bit because she looks like she's not sure if she's afraid of me again or not.

She's got me feeling so fucking high.

"I don't...do you know what an actuary is?"

"Like for an insurance company?"

"That's one path. I'm more interested in finance. But an actuary manages risk. That's what I am going to school for. That's what I do for internships. That's how I manage my life. And I realized that I'm going to be twenty-one in two days and have never tried to get into a bar. I know it sounds stupid, but I started feeling like I was having a mid-life crisis at twenty and just wanted to try something crazy. But not too crazy. Just crazy enough. Christa does it enough that I assumed it wasn't a big deal. That I could come in, look around, have a beer." She rubs her temple like maybe being young and dumb is giving her a headache. "She didn't tell me I might have to trade sexual favors." She meets my eyes. Doesn't look away. I know I'm big and scary to girls like her, but she doesn't look away. "I'm not going to have to trade sexual favors, am I?"

I've never forced a woman to do anything. I've never had to. My job is to ice bad situations, and sometimes that means protecting women from guys who aren't like me.

But who's going to protect my little actuary from me?

"You'll be begging me to fuck you before this night is over," I tell her. She hasn't responded to my crack about getting married yet. Maybe this will do it.

"You like to shock me."

"Yes."

"Why?"

A certainty moves through my chest. "Because you want to be shocked. That's why you're here tonight. You're not having a mid-life crisis. You're ready to grow up."

She rolls her eyes. "I've been grown-up for a long time, Mr. Anvil."

"You've been mature for a long time. I can see that. You don't have that teenage girl vibe around you. But you're aching to be treated like a real woman."

"Right. I'm going to call an Uber and go home now."

I step into her, blocking her against the desk, but I don't touch her. "Nothing wrong with wanting to be a woman. You're ready. I can feel it. Feel you in my blood."

She swallows hard. "That's not why I'm here. And you're scaring me."

"I'm not scaring you, angel. Your own desires are scaring you because they're new. Once you give in to them, you'll be changed. That scares the shit out of you." I lean down and smell the skin of her throat. *Mine*. "But you're not scared of me. We both know I'm not going to hurt you."

"How could I know that? You're like a wild animal compared to the boys I'm usually around."

Her pulse is going crazy, and I want to lick it. I want to taste every part of her. "I am a wild animal. But you can tame me."

"I doubt that very much."

"I want you to try."

"Is that why I'm still here? Why you didn't let me go? You want me to try to tame you?"

"You're here because you want to risk something tonight and still be safe. I'm the only man in this world who can make that happen for you. You can be as crazy as fuck. Do whatever you need to do, and I'll make sure you're safe. I'm the best risk averse choice you've ever made."

She can't read me yet. She doesn't know she's got all the control here. I'm already a fucking puppet for this woman. "So you want to be my bodyguard?"

"I won't let you out of my sight." I gently put my nose on that tender part under her ear but don't kiss her. "I'll be your actuary tonight, baby. I'll manage your risk."

She gives me a timid laugh. "This is crazy. I'm not having sex with you. If that's what you're after..."

"You saving it for marriage?" I ask

She tilts that proud little chin up and scoots away from me a bit. "Maybe I am."

"Then you'll be having sex with me before the night is through."

# Chapter Three

## Sarah

My life is officially out of control. My bodyguard let me have exactly one beer. And not in a bar. I got to drink it in his truck under his watchful eye about two hours ago. So I'm not drunk. I can't explain what is going on in my head, and I can't blame booze.

I think I'm drunk on him.

But when the officiant asks him if he takes me for better or worse, we both pause and look at each other like we just woke up from the world's strangest dream.

I guess a part of me thought I'd call his bluff at some point before now. He's taken me to several casinos and bars. He fed me a huge meal. He hasn't so much as kissed me. So when he suggested our next stop should be a 24-hour chapel, I laughed and said, "Sure. Why not?"

I've enjoyed living this one night free of worry. I can't explain it. Anvil makes me feel safe and shook up at the same time. Nothing, and I mean nothing, can hurt me. People clear a path for him wherever we go. He looks like we just left Thunderdome. He's a head taller than every other bouncer we've come across, and they haven't even carded me.

I have zero clue why he wants to hang out with me, though. I've seen the way women prettier than me look at him. Yeah, the scar, patch, and tattoos are scary, but in that primal way that makes us want what we shouldn't. He could have any of those women, probably at the same time. But he doesn't look at them. He looks at me. When I'm talking to him, he looks at me like I'm the smartest, most interesting person in the world. I don't get it.

While I am smart, I am not captivating. I understand that my chosen profession is not really exciting. But he kept asking me questions all night. But Anvil, he's the one with the good stories and exciting life. He's traveled so much. He was in the Army. He's got tales of adventure and anecdotes about funny and frightening bar fights.

And now we're in the chapel. The organist is smoking cigarettes. The officiant smells like wine coolers. Twelve hours ago, I ate a Hot Pocket while doing homework and now I'm getting married to a man I hardly know. But I said yes.

What kind of actuary am I going to be? This is more than risky.

"I do," Anvil says, and I feel relieved and inexplicably angry that he didn't cave in this game of chicken.

"You're insane," I whisper.

"You may kiss the bride," says the officiant. The organist starts and my husband...oh my God...my husband...smiles at me with the most devilish grin.

This will be our first kiss.

"Well, Mrs. Melvin Cartwright, I guess it's time to make this official."

His gaze moves to my mouth, and my lips part automatically, like he'd just said, "Open Sesame." His big calloused hand cups the curve of my jaw. Gently, so gently. He leans down so he's an inch from my other ear and smells my skin like he did back at Billy's.

I'm dying now. He's drawing this out so much. I'm about to just yell for him to kiss me already.

Then he claims my mouth. Finally. He brings his other hand up to hold my face, and I grasp his strong wrists so I don't fall over. His tongue sweeps into my mouth, and I moan. My skin tightens over my body, every nerve waiting for more touch, more sensation. But he doesn't go deeper. I try to angle my head to get more of him into me, but he holds us there in this sweet, sweet moment.

Oh my God, I'm married.

He leans his forehead on mine and looks into my eyes. I think it just hit him too. We're like two insane people inhabiting the bodies of normally rational people. Then he pulls me into his body, the shelter of his arms, and he holds me.

I didn't know. I never thought I could feel this way. I know I shouldn't fall for him. This isn't real. It's going to cost us an attorney fee tomorrow to figure out the best way to undo it. It's just my night of being rash. Of throwing caution into the wind.

But it feels good. It feels like the most real thing I've ever felt.

We're alone in the chapel now. The employees have gone out to get ready for the next insane couple.

He pulls back a little to look at me like he's looking through my skin and can see my darkest thoughts and my deepest longings. "I know, baby girl," he says. "Me too."

"Now what?" I ask, even though I know the answer. It's all been leading up to what comes next. I see that now.

"First, we get pancakes. Because I always celebrate the best things that happen to me with pancakes."

Okay, that wasn't what I thought he was going to say.

"Then I'm taking you home, and I'm going to fuck you hard and long and deep."

I inhale a shocked breath.

"I'm big everywhere, Mrs. Cartwright. We're gonna have to work to make it all fit in your virgin pussy. But you'll take all of me inside you, and you'll be mine."

I should be recoiling in horror. But I like what he's saying. I like the way he's saying it. The way he's looking at me like he's hungry for me.

For his wife.

"Are you wet? Are you thinking about my cock right now? Wondering how big it is? If I'm exaggerating?"

I nod. Well, I wanted to feel like I was alive and not just managing my life. Whatever happens tomorrow, I might as well give this night all the enthusiasm it's due. "I'm wet. I want you. I want you so much…I didn't know I could…" I drift off because I really don't know.

He saves me, stepping in when I get lost in my own words. "Woman, you are making me so hard right now. I'm going to make this so good for you. You'll be glad you waited for your wedding night, I promise."

"But first, pancakes," I say.

He smiles and I hear organ music that isn't playing. See fireworks that aren't exploding. I don't think he smiles very often. I feel like I just got a new super power that I can make him smile like that.

"First pancakes. Then you come all over my cock."

# Chapter Four

## Anvil

I sweep my bride into my arms at the threshold of my apartment so I can carry her in. It's cheesy as fuck, but this whole crazy night calls for it.

I'm married. What the hell? I don't know what I was thinking. I mean, yeah, I know I've been thinking with my dick all night. But if you'd have told me when I woke up this morning that I'd be somebody's husband before I went back to sleep tonight, I'd have beat you into thinking straight.

It's not sane, what I've done. This girl had plans. She's going somewhere in life and she doesn't need a bouncer holding her back. But she's my kind of trouble. And when she said she was saving herself for marriage, well, my brain disengaged from my dick.

At least, I'm blaming this on my dick.

I want to take her right to the bedroom and drop her in the center of my bed. But she's been getting quieter the closer we got to home, so I know her brain has started chattering at her. She's probably running graphs and pie charts and statistics in her head about how insane this is. What we've done. *The Bouncer and the Actuary* doesn't exactly sound like one of the Harlequin books my mom always had in her purse when I was a kid.

Mom. Hell. She's going to love Sarah. But first, she's going to kill me for getting married without her. And I don't know anything about Sarah's family, but I'm guessing this isn't going to be their favorite news either. Funny how none of that occurred to me while I stood in front of her and promised her my future.

I ease her onto her feet. She immediately wraps her arms around herself. She's stiff and uncomfortable. That's not how I want this to go.

"Baby, what's wrong?"

Her eyebrows reach for her forehead. "What's wrong? What isn't wrong? What did we do? What are we doing?"

"We'll figure it out as we go," I promise.

"That's not how I work, Anvil." She lets go of her middle and starts pacing. "I don't do this. I plan things out, each step. I don't elope with strangers. I don't go home with strangers. I don't have sex with strangers. This is not who I am. I don't even know how I caught your interest, but I think you're going to be pretty disappointed when you figure out that the last few hours are not the real me."

"Stop," I warn. And she shuts up and looks at me.

"Nobody forced you to say *I do*, baby. You were right there with me. It's crazy, I'll give you that. But telling me that it isn't you is a lie. Maybe you only detour from your plans once in a while, but it's still you. And now that you're married, you don't have to worry about getting crazy and eloping with strangers again."

She barks out a little laugh. "You're crazy."

I take her hand and lead her to the couch. "Yeah, probably. But if you're worried about it, you're the first time I've eloped with a stranger, too. I've never gotten close to an altar before, baby. I never thought I would get married."

"So why me? I saw the way women look at you. I'm sure I'm not your type."

I trace patterns on her hand and arm with my fingers. "I don't have a lot of words for you." She relaxes a little. "I'm not good at romance. I saw you, and then you were all I could see."

"Oh," she breathes out like she's a little surprised. "That's actually very romantic."

"Why'd you pick me? We both know I'm not your type."

She brings one of my hands into her small ones. I'm like a fucking giant near her. I don't know how I ever got her to leave Billy's with me, much less back to my house as my wife. She's very serious now, studying my hand, stroking hers over it. Like she's learning me. "I'm probably not much better at words than you are. I was starting to feel so restless and uneasy. I know I need organization and plans to feel good and safe. But I think I'm going too far. Or I was. I wasn't living life, I was living a plan. I needed to shake things up. And then you came in, and I felt a different kind of restless and a different kind of safe. Like—I don't know—like finally it was starting."

"What was starting?"

She shrugs. "I don't know. It's crazy. I feel like I have stage fright, I'm nervous. But it's a good kind of nervous. Like I'm doing something big."

Yeah. She'll be doing something big pretty soon. But I don't tell her that.

"If we were smart, we'd stop this right now," she says, and all the air is sucked from the room, from my lungs. "It will be easier to annul if I go home and we let a lawyer fix this."

She dares to meet my eyes. I can't tell what she wants me to say or do.

"Is that what you want?"

"It's the smart thing to do. The way of less risk."

"I didn't ask that. I asked what you want." I'm not a guy of tenderness and patience. I give what I deem to be justice at the time and take what I deem to be mine when I want it. She's a virgin. Inexperienced. She was looking for a beer tonight, and I've changed everything.

I pull her across me so she's straddling my lap. She gives a little mew and her eyes get real big and round. I pull her arms behind her, grasping both wrists in one hand so she has to lean forward to balance. She can feel my cock beneath her. No way she can't. It's hard as stone with her this close…and growing.

"Do you want to forget this night? Chalk it up to some crazy memory you have of college?" My other hand goes behind her neck, grasping her nape and pulling her face closer to me. "Or do you want to know how it feels to be my woman? Do you want my cock deep inside you? Do you want me to claim you? Make you come?" She squirms as she blushes, and the friction of her on my cock is delicious and painful at the same time. There's little space between our faces now. She can see the scar up close, but it's the intensity in my eye that's causing her to shiver. "You need to decide, baby. I want to make you my wife. But you have to think like a woman, not a girl. You ready for that?"

"I don't know."

So I let go. She makes a whimper in the back of her throat as I sit all the way back against the couch cushion. She has to catch herself with her hands on my chest, the angle sliding her pussy against my cock again. Christ.

"Wait, don't...don't let go. Don't give up on me," she pleads. She rolls her hips and gasps. Yeah, I feel it too. Like a million volts of electricity arcing between us wherever we touch. "I'm just nervous. I don't know what to do or how to act. I don't even know where to put my hands."

"You don't need to be experienced as long as you're enthusiastic," I say. I slide my hand to the center of her back and push her onto my chest. Her head is resting above my heart. "But I'm not playing games. Either you want this or you don't."

She lifts her head. "I want this."

"Tell me more," I say. "Once we start, I can't pull back. Not with you. I know it already. I won't take what's not mine, angel, but once you give yourself to me, I'm taking it all. I won't stop. I won't ever stop. You'll be taking my cock any way I give it to you, wherever and whenever."

"I can't tell if you're trying to warn me off you or seduce me," she says.

"You're still on my fucking lap, so I think you like it when I tell you what I want to do to you."

She nods her head a little, her cheeks stained pink. "I think maybe I do."

"Then tell me so I understand. What do you want, Sarah Cartwright?"

She places a soft kiss on my chest above my heart that almost kills me. "I want you. I want this. Make me yours. Wife me, Anvil."

# Chapter Five

## Sarah

The noise he makes is a feral growl and it ignites something inside me that I've never felt before. Never knew I could feel.

I'm still trying to process what I just said, what I just gave him permission...no, invitation...to do to me when he yanks me up to his mouth. I thirst for him, opening my mouth to drink him in. I'm completely flattened against his hard muscles, and he squeezes me like he's trying to push me into and under his skin as his mouth takes mine. His tongue begins basically fucking my mouth, and I'm trapped in his arms as if I were tied up and I love it. I give in to the dominance of his kiss. The dominance of him. He's so hard and hot and strong, he becomes my entire world.

He snakes his hand down the back of my pants and squeezes my ass, pushing and grinding me against his erection. There's probably no way that monster will even fit. But there's a hollowness inside me, low and achy. It's pulling at my insides, growing bigger like a black hole. I need to be filled. I need him inside me to fill the hollow.

"Fuck, you're going to make me come in my pants," he says, taking a break from bruising my mouth as he goes to my throat. His stubble is grazing my neck and his teeth are biting my skin. "Wife me, she says. Fuck. Why is that so fucking hot?"

I don't know.

He's my husband. I'm *married* to him. My pussy floods with wetness at the thought. I belong to him. But maybe what's getting me so hot is realizing that he belongs to me. Mine. He's all mine.

I've made out with guys before and it was nothing like this. Anvil is primal and is stripping me down to my core animal. And he's mine. The idea of him, of this, of us...I can't fathom now how I made it this far in life without it. I feel like I was made to be his wife. How is that even possible? We just met.

"I want to see you," I say. Which for me, might be the most brazen thing I've ever said. But I want to touch his skin. Taste him. I lean back to make room for him to take off his shirt. My God, he's beautiful.

His chest is broad, of course. Lined with bulging muscles. He's got thick hair at the center of his pecs that tapers down like a tour guide to his abs then lower still, drawing my eyes to the waistband of his jeans. I run my fingers through it. It's course yet soft. I follow the path up and down with my hand; his skin seems to jump under my touch. I lean down and tongue the flat disc of his nipple and he moans, clutching my head there in case I move away too fast.

"That's good, baby. Oh fuck, that's good." The fact that I'm giving him pleasure turns me on more than I already was—and I didn't think that was possible.

But he's impatient and his hands pull up on the hem of my shirt, so I lift my arms to get it off me. My bra is plain and boring. I didn't know it would be my wedding night when I got dressed to go out. He flicks the front closure and it pops open, my breasts popping free like the biscuit dough in a can. His eye gets darker, dilating, and then the world shifts and I'm on my back and he's sucking one of my breasts while he grinds into my pelvis.

I cry out, the sensations pulling inside me like dark secrets. He keeps grinding, sucking, biting, and I feel like I'm falling, faster and faster. Racing toward the ground. My hands fist in his hair and I cry out as I come. My first time with someone in the room with me.

He pulls back, his chin on my stomach, my skin stretching and puckering into goose bumps from the rough stubble. "I could get addicted to the sound you make when you come, angel. I think I need to hear it again." He's undoing the button of my jeans, yanking my pants down and off my legs. He puts his nose right into my panty-covered pussy and inhales deeply. "Oh yeah. That's so good. Mmmm."

I want to cover myself with my hand. Push his nose away. It's too much. He's making me feel too many things at once. Shock. Modesty. Fear. Anticipation.

He pulls the material over, exposing me to him, and dabs his tongue right into my slit. I arch like a current of electricity has just electrocuted me, the aftershocks still coming from my first orgasm. The shock and modesty melt away pretty quickly, to be honest. All that's left is the fear and anticipation, and those two feelings play off each other in an interesting harmony that keeps me turned on.

I look down at the juncture of my thighs to find him watching my face.

"I'm going to wear this pretty little cunt out tonight." He's looking into my eyes, seeing how far he can go with his dirty talk. To find where I draw the line. Do I have a line? I don't think I do. Not with him. Not with my husband. "You're wet, angel. So wet for me. For my tongue and my fingers and my dick."

I nod.

One yank and my panties are torn off. He pushes my legs wide apart. "Look at that pretty pussy. All creamy and juicy." He spreads my lips apart. "I'm going to suck on that sweet, creamy clit of yours. Every last drop. My mouth is watering, angel."

And then I'm moaning as he kisses my pussy the way he took my mouth earlier. He's tongue fucking me, his thumb on my clit. I should be embarrassed at the sounds I am making. The way I'm grinding against his face. But I'm not. I'm fucking free.

"You make me so greedy, baby. I love drinking your sweet juices down. The more I eat you, the harder I get.

He latches on again. I lose track of my orgasms. When he finally pulls away from me, I'm almost relieved at the break. I hear his zipper, so I raise up on my elbows to see him.

Oh.

My.

God.

"Yeah, sweetness. Look at my cock. Baby, what have you gotten yourself in to?" He rests his cock on my mound. It's the size of my forearm and so heavy against me. "See how hard it is for you. See what you do to me? My face is fucking covered in your girl come and my dick wants some too." He taps it on my pussy. "You were such a good girl before you met me, weren't you?"

I nod, mesmerized by the beast oozing pre-come from the mushroom tip. It's porno big. And I don't think there's room inside me for both of us, I really don't. But when he slides it through the lips of my pussy, my juices combining with his to let it glide smooth, I feel that hollowness inside again. There is only one thing that will ease the ache. I know it and he knows it.

He pushes my legs back and rest them on his shoulders. Then he pulls my arms until they are pinned above my head, my wrists in his hand. With his other hand, he adjusts the angle of his cock so just the tip is poised at my entrance. He leans forward, pressuring the head in.

"That feels so good already, baby." He turns his face into my legs and kisses it tenderly. "Your pussy is grabbing my cock so tightly, honey."

My legs start shaking as he works in a little more. I move my hips as the sensation of being filled too much increases.

"You on the pill, honey?"

How could I have forgotten about condoms? I shake my head. "No, we need..." He pushes in a little more, and I forget what I was saying.

"I don't want anything between us," he says.

Alarm bells jangle in my brain. "But—"

"Look at me," he commands. His face is red, pinched with lust for me. "I kept you safe all night, yeah?" I nod. "I promise you, I'm clean. I've never had sex without a condom. Not once. And I get tested regularly. I would never endanger you. Do you believe me?"

God help me, I do. "But—"

"Babies aren't in your five-year-plan. I get it. Neither was a husband."

His fingers do magical things to my clit while he talks, rendering me unable to think. "I want to fill you with my come, Sarah. I want to come inside you over and over." He pushes all the way in and pauses, letting me adjust to the pain, the fullness. "That's it, baby. Relax and get used to my cock."

My breath comes hard and fast, the pain blinding at first. I blink rapidly as it begins to fade, like I'm coming to. And there he is, watching me closely, rubbing his bearded face on my leg while he waits patiently for me to relax again.

I'm not a virgin anymore.

And I somehow made it to my wedding day as one.

And I married the scariest man I've ever seen. Who I believe in my heart will protect me and do anything to make me happy. I don't have enough data to make that judgement. I don't have facts or comps or anything but what my untried heart is telling me.

I'm completely open to him. My arms and legs immobile. "I need you to kiss me," I whisper.

He maneuvers my limbs around his waist and he takes my mouth. I rock my hips up, now aching to get closer. It hurts a little again, but he soothes it when he starts moving. Slowly at first, as he pulls back and hisses with pleasure when he eases back in.

"You feel so fucking good." He starts playing with my clit again. "I need you to come around my cock this time, baby. I need it so bad. You're so tight. So sweet."

I don't have any defense for this. For his words. For his fat cock. For the way every inch of me feels full. I start coming again, only this time, I don't think I will ever stop.

"You're milking my cock, angel. You're going to pull all my come out of me, aren't you? You want it inside you?"

He's on the edge of coming. I haven't stopped. He should pull out. I should tell him to pull out. Instead, I dig my heels into his back, locking my legs around him, pulling him deeper into my body. "Make me yours."

He freezes, shaking with his need as he stares at me to be sure. He lets go of my wrists so he can angle my hips and he starts thrusting like he's trying to fuck me through to the box spring of his bed. "My horny girl wants to be bred on her first ride," he grunts out. "Gonna give her everything she wants." One final thrust and he curses as his warm seed shoots into me. He clutches my hips in those big hands, holding me still to accept all his come. As his cock throbs, I have another orgasm, drawing him deeper into my body.

We lay like this for a long time. Until the sweat on my body chills. Until I begin to feel sore where his cock still remains.

"Never letting you go now, babe," he says. "I think I was unconscious there for a minute."

"Me too," I say.

He takes me to his shower and sweetly cleans me up. Then he carries me back to his bed...our bed...and we fall asleep until noon.

I'm certainly not feeling restless anymore.

The rest of the day, we eat, make love, and eat some more. He tells me how he lost his eye. About his business plan for a bar of his own. At midnight, he takes me to Billy's Suds for my first legal drink.

It's weird, getting to know my husband after the wedding instead of before it. But I have a feeling he's worth the risk.

# Epilogue

## Anvil

*Two Years Later*

My wife will be home from work in half an hour and the house is a disaster. I'm trying to keep it clean as we go, but our daughter is a holy terror since she learned to walk a few months ago.

I'm Mr. Mom, and if you think it's funny now, you should have seen how funny it was the first time I took Kayla, our baby, to Mommy and Me swimming lessons. We've ironed out the rough spots. When Sarah was still in school, I worked nights at Billy's. But once she got the new job, it made more sense for me to stay home. I'm not worried about fragile masculinity for damn sure. Someone else has a problem with it, I still have anvils for fists. They can take it up with them.

I like my life just fine.

We talk about opening the bar someday with what I've saved, but for now, I don't want to be away from my family at night. I want to protect them, be with them. And fuck my wife every night after the baby goes to sleep.

I pop Kayla in a playpen and do the best I can with the house. By the time Sarah gets home, the pancake batter is ready for her birthday celebration.

When we get Kayla to sleep that night, I pull my wife into bed.

"C'mon Mrs. Cartwright, it's time to put another deposit down on baby number two."

"It's my birthday, I get what I want. And what I want is your dick in my mouth."

Can't argue with the lady. It's her birthday, after all.

She's got me right where she wants me after just a few minutes of that talented tongue and her warm mouth. "Babe, c'mon. I don't want to waste it in your mouth. Let me have your pussy."

I'm so hot thinking about getting her knocked up again. Fuck, she was so pretty all round with my baby.

"You don't want me to swallow your come?" she asks after taking my dick out of her mouth. She's tapping it against her cheek. Her skin is flushed and her lips red and swollen. So damn pretty.

"Another time. I want to get you pregnant. Now put your toy down and get over here."

She smiles. "You can't get me pregnant tonight. Might as well let me finish you here."

"That sounds like a challenge. Let me try to get you pregnant anyway."

She shakes her head. "You can't."

I sit up. "Why not?"

She moves up the bed, straddling my cock and easing down on it. "Because I already am pregnant. I took a test on my lunch hour today."

I pull her as close to me as I can, and she fucks me slowly. "I love you so much, baby."

"I love you, too."

People thought we were crazy. They told us to give up back then. Get the annulment. Be reasonable. The bouncer and the actuary. What did we have in common? We didn't even know each other. We'd never last.

I squeeze my wife, my world, tighter to me. My whole fucking world.

---

I KNOW THAT WAS SUPER crazy, right? Instalove. Over-the-top. Unrealistic as hell. Did you love Anvil and Sarah, though? That combination of sweet and filthy? The primal caveman who is a total Alphamallow? There's more where that came from. The **Blue Collar Bad Boy** series is just beginning. Sign up for Brill's Bites[1] so you never miss a new release. Sexy bad boys who do sexy bad things with their rough hands and the innocent virgins who love them. What's not to like?

Here is a peek of the next story about the carpenter and the *Jeopardy* nerd...*Nailed*

---

1. http://eepurl.com/cP0AZr

# Nailed

**BRILL HARPER**

# CHAPTER ONE

## Megan

WHEN THE CARPENTER knocked on the door, I was expecting someone else. I mean, I knew a carpenter was coming, I just didn't expect someone like *him*. I figured someone older. But Brody Maines isn't old. He's older than my nineteen years, but probably only by five or so.

I'm holding my ginormous science textbook in front of me like a shield. Not that it could help much—neither the book itself or the knowledge inside can help me now.

I'm over my head.

Brody is a big man—he has to be over six-feet-tall by three or four inches, and his muscles look like they are currently trying to tear out of his t-shirt. From a scientific perspective, which is usually my only perspective, he's an excellent specimen of the male species. His waist-to-chest ratio affirms the correct V shape to indicate a higher level of testosterone and correlating dominance. His square jaw and ridged brow also indicate that he is likely in high demand as a mating partner.

While my knowledge of biology is strong, it is not helping me communicate at this moment. I am better with books than people. But the books are right when it comes to sexual selection. I want to have this man's babies just by looking at him.

We stand in the doorway, me on one side, him on the other, an awkward silence filling the space between. Instead of forming actual words, all I can do is blink up at him.

Way, way up.

He is all man in a way an inexperienced girl like me, even with my lack of people skills, knows is trouble. He radiates power and a kind of dominance that makes me weak in the knees. I feel overpowered by his presence, but I *want* to be overpowered. It is quite disconcerting.

His eyes are gray, no that's not right. They're too dark to be called gray. Maybe charcoal is a better description. And they are focused on me.

I really should be saying something. Like "hello" or "come in."

But I get sidetracked by his hair. It's thick and a color that's not blond, but not brown either. It appears to be silky soft. It occurs to me that I've never touched another person's hair. In all the years I've been alive—that can't be right can it?

Yes, I suppose it is.

My father is not affectionate with me. Or perhaps I am not affectionate with my father. I love him. But we're not close that way. And I have never been the slumber party kind of girl, so no hair braiding with my friends. And well, my lack of hair touching opportunities with boys in high school was not a surprise to me or the boys I went to school with.

College has turned out no differently at this point.

I'm just an odd girl. I always have been. I'm too serious. Too studious. And too introverted to break out of that mold now.

So if Brody's hair looks silky soft to me, I don't have prior experience to base that on. It's just a hypothesis.

I have a lot of those. Unanswered suppositions.

His eyebrows are drawing together like he's confused. Which is my fault because I'm handling answering the door in a very weird way. Trust that I can take any situation and turn it into something awkward. It's a gift.

His cheek bones are sharp, his nose a little crooked, but his lips make my insides flutter. The bottom one is plumper than the top, and it makes me want to bite it. Since I've never bitten anyone before, nor had the urge to, I don't know why it feels like instinct.

Bringing my gaze down, it lands on his hands. They are massive. They look so strong. Like he could crush things with them, but I know, instead, he uses them to create things. Beautiful things. My dad, who is by nature a collector of beautiful things, hired Brody to put a built-in desk in his office like the one he saw at his friend's home office. My dad didn't care how much it cost. He didn't even try to negotiate. That is unusual. Not his competition to one up his friend—that's normal for my dad. It's the not negotiating a price down part that is off his normal baseline behavior. He must really want that desk. I saw pictures of some of

Brody's pieces, and he is an artist with a good reputation for his work.

I bet he has a bad reputation though, too. I can't stop thinking about how his rough fingers would feel on my untouched skin. I'm getting wet and it's embarrassing. This getting wet thing is a bit new to me as I've only started recently. Delayed onset of sexuality has hindered my ability to fit in with my peers for years. And now that it's here, I don't have anyone to talk to about it. People my age have been dealing with this for a long time. It would be strange for me to approach someone about it anyway.

Brody looks at me like I'm a wild animal he's trying to coax out of a trap. He puts his hands in front of him so I can see them. He inclines his head to look less aggressive. "You're Megan, right? Did your dad forget to tell you I was coming? I can wait out here while you call him."

"Uh." *Speak, Megan. Speak.* I'm just dumbstruck. Which is ironic considering my brains are really my only asset.

"You okay?" His jaw squares like he's clenching it, and he looks beyond my shoulder into the house. "Are you afraid of me or is something else scaring you? Is someone in your house?"

Before I can tell him nothing is wrong but my inability to act like a normal person in the presence of a male of my species, he pushes past me, blocking me between the doorway and his ridiculously large body. He smells like sawdust and evergreen.

Nobody has ever offered to stand between me and trouble before. I've never felt so safe or protected. I file the feeling away to investigate again later. When my heart slows and I resume measured breathing and can think straight. Likely not until Brody leaves.

"I'm fine," I answer, closing the door and leaning against it. "There's nothing going on in here. I'm just a dork."

He turns, his gaze taking me in from head to toe. His eyes seem to push into me, pulling out secrets. I can't catch my breath.

Wow. He is just *wow*. So intense, so ruggedly handsome. And burly. He takes up so much room as he dominates the space around him.

"Why do you think you're a dork?" he asks finally.

I shrug. Perhaps he knows nothing about fashion, because one look at my outfit could probably answer that for him. But that's not all. "I don't have a lot of social skills."

He shrugs back. "I don't like people much either."

"It's not that I don't like people. I just don't know how to act around them. I say stupid things." Like now. "It's worse with boys."

"Good thing I'm not a boy then."

That sounds like flirting. Is he flirting with me? I can't be sure. It is the closest I've ever come to flirting though.

Who am I kidding? No guy with biceps that thick would flirt with me. My stupid hormones. I don't know what to do with all these new feelings he's churned up inside me. Because suddenly, I can picture what it would be like to be under him. To have all his attention on me. To be completely filled by him.

Heat pulses between my legs in time with my heart. I am achy and wet and this has never, ever happened to me so strongly before.

The room is so hot. Or maybe it's just me. I'm burning up. I feel needy and want things I don't know how to name.

Maybe after he leaves, I'll visit that porn site again. I've been trying to understand sex. Textbooks only go so far. It's not like

I'm getting much help from guys my own age. They're like this whole other alien species to me. I can observe them, make what I think are reasonable deductions about their behavior, but the interacting part never seems to go the way I think it will.

I hear girls talking about sex like it's this great thing, but until Brody knocked on my door, I never felt the sexual attraction they would discuss. Perhaps now that my body has responded this way to an actual person, the porn clips will make more sense. I want to learn how to be aroused and cause arousal in someone else. This will probably require that I spend time outside of class doing things other than studying.

So tonight, after Brody leaves, instead of spending my evening reading the new book I bought about world history, I will try to masturbate while thinking of Brody. My hypothesis is that the way he makes me feel standing here while he is fully clothed will still stimulate me later when I allow myself to imagine him naked. If that is true, then I will once again get wet, and this time when I stimulate my clitoris, I will be able to achieve an orgasm.

It will be my first.

It occurs to me that I am applying the scientific method to making myself come and that perhaps this is why nobody has shown any interest in me as of yet. I am not able to just let go, stop thinking. I don't think it's an attractive trait to young men. Or maybe any men.

Masturbating while thinking of Brody and watching pornographic images is probably as close as this girl will ever get to sexual satisfaction.

# About the Author

Like first times? Forbidden fruit?
Yes, please.
Love a hot, dominant alpha claiming what's his?
Fuck, yeah.
Want to watch him fall hard for the sweetest fantasy he didn't know he needed?
Me too!
I'm Brill Harper and I love happily ever afters, smokin' hot bad boys, and quirky heroines that I'd love to be friends with off page. These ladies are not perfect—but they're perfect for one man—and he's always sexy AF.
Seriously—these heroes only have one weakness, and it's sticky, sweet love. They don't let anything stand in the way of taking what belongs to them. When it comes to the woman they love, it's hard cocks, dirty talk, and soft, mushy heart feels. I like to call them Alphamallows.

* Brill Harper is a pseudonym. Like...a secret identity. By day she's Clark Kent, writing romance books for young adults and grownups. By night, she's Brill Harper writing unfailingly filthy, yet super sweet books, that would make her alter ego blush.

<u>www.brillharper.com</u>[1]
Facebook [2] | Brill's Bites[3]

---

1. http://www.brillharper.com

2. https://www.facebook.com/Brill-Harper-1931520800417566/

3. http://eepurl.com/cP0AZr

# Don't miss out!

Visit the website below and you can sign up to receive emails whenever Brill Harper publishes a new book. There's no charge and no obligation.

https://books2read.com/r/B-A-XQLE-GFAP

BOOKS 2 READ

Connecting independent readers to independent writers.

# Also by Brill Harper

**Blue Collar Bad Boys**
Bounced: A Blue Collar Bad Boys Book
Nailed: A Blue Collar Bad Boys Book
Drilled: A Blue Collar Bad Boys Book
Wrecked: A Blue Collar Bad Boys Book
Laid: A Blue Collar Bad Boys Book
Tagged: A Blue Collar Bad Boys Christmas
Plowed: A Blue Collar Bad Boys Book
Bucked: A Blue Collar Bad Boys Book
Banged: A Blue Collar Bad Boys Book
Tapped: A Blue Collar Bad Boy Book

**Standalone**
Blue Collar Bad Boys Volume 1: Books 1-3
Blue Collar Bad Boys Volume 2: Books 4-6
Dirty Jobs: a Blue Collar Bad Boys Collection
Notch on His Bedpost
Altogether

Watch for more at www.brillharper.com.

Printed in Great Britain
by Amazon